DATE DUE

GAYLORD		PRINTED IN U.S.A.

tofu quilt

tofu quilt

by ching yeung russell

楊青

LEE & LOW BOOKS INC.
New York

LEE & LOW BOOKS Inc., 95 Madison Avenue, New York, NY 10016

leeandlow.com

Manufactured in the United States of America

Book design by Kimi Weart

Book production by The Kids at Our House

The text is set in Centaur

10 9 8 7 6 5 4 3 2 1

First Edition

Library of Congress Cataloging-in-Publication Data

Russell, Ching Yeung.

Tofu quilt / by Ching Yeung Russell. — 1st ed.

p. cm.

Summary: Growing up in 1960s Hong Kong, a young girl dreams of becoming a writer in spite of conventional limits placed on her by society and family.

ISBN 978-1-60060-423-2 (alk. paper)

1. Hong Kong (China)—History—20th century—Juvenile fiction. [1. Novels in verse.
2. Hong Kong (China)—History—20th century—Fiction. 3. Authorship—Fiction.
4. Sex role—Fiction.] I. Title.

PZ7.5.R87To 2009

[Fic]—dc22   2009016903

to the memory of uncle five,
who provided me with an education in China.

to my mother,
who never told me to change jobs
when I struggled with my writing career.

to the memory of my father,
whose tofu quilts gave me inspiration.

to my brother and sisters,
Patrick Yeung, Lily Kam, and Rita Nishimura.
We are always a family.

to candie ruppert,
my teacher friend who reads my books
to her fourth grade students each year.

contents

tofu quilt

the joy of summer

Ma and I take a train from Hong Kong
to the nearby city of Guangzhou
on the Mainland
to stay for a few days with Uncle Five,
one of Ma's brothers.

I hide in the washroom
the day we plan to go back home.
Ma finally agrees to let me stay longer.
She will pick me up

at the end of the summer,

before I start kindergarten.

Like a little duck,

I follow a group of cousins, boys and girls,

wherever they go.

I am always behind,

running and trying to catch up, calling,

"Wait for me! Wait for me!"

Some days

we jump into the pond

behind our plaza.

While everybody else races,

swimming toward the big rock

in the middle of the pond

to claim the title of King or Queen of the Pond,

I hold on to the rocky shore

and kick the water,

as content as

a puppy learning a new trick.

Some days

we climb up

into the giant banyan tree

next to the pond,

pretending we are Tarzan

calling to his animals.

The giant banyan tree

bursts into a laughing tree.

For one of us sounds like a chicken

whose neck has just been slit;

one sounds like a pig being hauled to the butcher;

one sounds like a stray cat begging for food;

one sounds like a goat running in the rain.

I sound like a chick peeping for its ma.

Still,

each claims that his or her sound is what Tarzan yells.

None of us really knows,

since my cousin only read it in a book.

Some days we go to the small ditch

beside the vegetable patch

to hunt for water snakes.

We tie an old, mended trap net onto a stick

and hang it across the ditch

to trap the snake in the net

as it swims by.

I turn my head away

as my cousin skins the snake.

The meat is for soup,

and he sells the skin to

a musical instrument maker

to cover the head of a *yee wu*.

Some days

we don't do anything.

We sit idly on the ground in the shady, narrow alley

between two gray brick houses

to cool off

and tell jokes and just be silly.

I am not Queen of the Pond.

I cannot trap any snakes.

But I do not mind

being a little duck,

always calling

"Wait for me! Wait for me!"

somersault

In the evenings, after supper,
Uncle Five gathers all my cousins,
seven of them,
and sits at a round table
with a kerosene lamp in the middle.

He teaches my cousins
classical poems
as I do somersaults all by myself
on the hardwood bed
next to them.

I have fun watching my cousins

dozing off

as Uncle Five recites the poems

with his eyes closed

behind his glasses

and his head tilted up slightly,

as if he is singing a song.

Once

Uncle Five tells me to be quiet,

but I can't sit still.

I keep rolling around on the bed until

I blurt out a whole poem

to help Cousin Yee,

who is trying to recite the poem

from memory,

struggling,

as if she is trying to pull a buffalo

up a tree.

Uncle Five

never tells me to sit still

again.

For I, a five-year-old child,

can beat my older cousins

at reciting all the poems,

even though I don't know what they

mean.

a bowl of *dan lai*

To reward me
for reciting many poems from memory,
Uncle Five takes my cousins and me
to another town,
for my first bowl of *dan lai*
before I go back to Hong Kong.

To get to the town,
we ride in a sampan,
which takes half a day
just for one way.

I wonder why Uncle Five

is bringing us so far.

Dan lai must be

a very special reward.

When the waiter brings us the dan lai,

it looks like a big, round moon

has fallen into my bowl.

Its surface is as smooth as

my baby sister's bottom.

Its color is as creamy as

Pau Pau's ivory chopsticks.

I can't even describe

the special sweet smell,

but I just keep sniffing it,

like a hungry wolf.

The dan lai looks so perfect that

I don't want to stir it,

even though my stomach is rumbling
like a faraway thunderstorm.
I keep swallowing my saliva
as I watch my cousins
enjoy their dan lai,
spoonful by spoonful.

I can't stand it any longer.
Even though it is still hot
and burns my mouth,
I gobble up the whole moon
as fast as a strong wind sweeping away clouds.
I hope Uncle Five will get me another bowl,
like we refill our rice bowl
at every meal.
But Uncle Five says, "Wait until another time."

I don't drink any tea afterward,
fearing it will wash away

the sweetness in my mouth.
And I don't brush my teeth
before going to bed,
hoping to savor the taste
of dan lai forever
and ever.

home again

Early in the morning the day after she arrives
at Uncle Five's house on the Mainland,
Ma takes me home.
I wave to my cousins
as they watch the train slowly move
like a snail crawling
with its heavy shell.
The *chik chor, chik chor* sound of the engine
echoes in the morning breeze.

Soon my cousins are out of sight,
as houses and trees speed backward.

I rest my chin in my hand,

my elbow on the train's windowsill.

I am sad

and happy at the same time,

like eating a bowl of sweet and sour soup.

Ma breaks the silence

by saying,

"I know you had fun

just by looking at your suntan;

you're as dark as charcoal.

Tell me what you liked the most."

"Dan lai!" I burst out.

"I wish Uncle Five

would have let me eat more than one bowl.

I didn't have enough."

"It's very expensive," Ma says.

"Why?" I ask. "It's just a small bowl."

"Dan lai is the specialty of the town," she says.

"And it is only made

from one family's secret recipe."

"Have *you* tried it?" I ask Ma.

"Yes," she says. "A long time ago."

I promise Ma,

"When I grow up,

after I get rich,

I will buy you a bowl of dan lai!"

Ma smiles.

"After you start going to school,

you will learn many things.

And you will be rich in many ways."

"Then I can buy a bowl of dan lai for everyone

in the family," I boast.

"Yes, you can, as long as you stay in school."

"I want to go to school now!" I say.

"I can't wait!"

As the train gets close to Hong Kong,
I can hardly wait to hug Pau Pau.
I can hardly wait to see Ba Ba.
I can hardly wait to play with
my sister, my brother, and the baby.

Now I am just happy,
like when I eat a bowl of
cold, sweet red bean porridge
on a hot summer day.

braiding my hair

After I get home,
I go to see Pau Pau, my ma's ma.
She lives with Uncle Seven
and his family,
about a block from where we live.
Pau Pau is so pleased
when I tell her what Uncle Five did
with my cousins and me.

"Not too hard! It hurts!" I cry
while Pau Pau combs the tangles out of my hair.

She teases me,

"Your scalp is as soft as tofu.

But your hair is as coarse as your ma's.

No wonder you and she are so stubborn."

"Is stubborn good?" I ask.

"Good for a boy. Not good for a girl," she says.

"Boys need to be stubborn

so they can succeed."

"What about girls?" I ask.

"Girls shouldn't be stubborn," she says.

"They need to listen to their parents

when they are little.

They need to listen to their husbands

after they get married."

"I don't want to be a girl," I declare.

"I want to be a boy!"

Pau Pau bursts out laughing.

"You sound just like your ma

when she was little!"

my ba ba, the tailor

My ba ba is a tailor.

He works in a big, well-known clothing shop.

He is the best

of all the workers

at assembling the collar and lapels—

the eyes of a suit.

The boss asks only Ba Ba to make all the

white dinner jackets

for his *kwailo* customers.

Ba Ba doesn't brag,

but I know he is proud
from the way he hums at home.

Ba Ba can look at my friends' clothes
and make me clothes exactly like they have
just by drawing lines on material
and cutting out the pieces.
His feet pump out a steady
cha cha cha on the sewing machine treadle,
and he finishes my clothes
as quickly as I can blink my eyes.

But Ba Ba is often short of cash
for buying material.
That's why we,
the tailor's children—
all four of us—
wear clothes
made from his old shirts

and Ma's clothes that no longer fit.

Ma often says,

"Nobody would believe

that a tailor who works as hard as a water buffalo

has children with no new clothes."

the wish

I am the first child in my family.

When I was born,

Ah Mah, my ba ba's ma, said to Ba Ba,

"You still have a chance for a boy."

My sister is the second child.

When she was born,

Ma said, "Girls and boys are just the same."

Ah Mah does not say a word.

But she is getting worried,

and so is Ba Ba.

They worry that child number three

will also be a girl

and that there will be no boy

to carry on our family name

and no one to take care of them

when they grow old.

Ba Ba dresses my sister

like a boy

hoping that this will

bring a boy to my family,

until finally my brother is born.

my ma, rebel of the yeung family

My ma is a big, tall woman, like a Northerner,
not a Cantonese.
She went to school for many years
when she was young.
She always quotes from the Chinese classics
when she argues with Ba Ba
or gives us a lecture
with her "three-inch tongue."
Just by listening to the way she talks
people know

she is highly educated,

unlike most of the women

her age.

Uncle Five told me

Ma could calculate with an abacus

as swiftly and accurately as he could.

She manipulated the beads

with only her thumb and middle finger,

sending out a steady

tak tak, tok tok

like a machine gun

shooting out the numbers

so fast,

so loud,

so accurate.

This was before she married Ba Ba,

when she helped in Uncle Five's store

in their hometown in mainland China.

Ma is the one

Ba Ba's older brothers and sisters

criticize the most,

because we don't own a flat

and sometimes we don't have enough money

for daily expenses

but she still sends me

to a private school.

They ask, "Why doesn't she send her daughter

to an inexpensive public school?

Why doesn't she send her

to be someone's babysitter

like we do with our girls,

so she can help pay for a flat.

After a girl is married off,

she is like a bucket of water

being poured out!

Ba Ba is often speechless
in front of his brothers and sisters.
But Ma is hopping mad
after Ba Ba tells her what they said.
She proclaims,
"I don't gamble like some of them!
I don't waste any of my money!
I send my daughter to private school
and have no shame
in front of your Yeung ancestors!"

That's why we are the poorest,
but the richest,
of all the Yeungs.
Because of my ma,
the rebel
of the Yeung family.

our next-door neighbor
mrs. ho

In the summertime,
Mrs. Ho, who lives on our hall
in our seven-story apartment building,
walks along the long corridor
with her baby on her back,
door-to-door,
being friendly with everyone
at suppertime.

She wants to see
what kind of food

each family has for supper.

She peers through the iron security gates,

looking into every one-room flat

to decide

if that family has money for food.

When Ma is short of money,

from paying rent and school fees,

we eat only vegetables and salty dried fish.

We close the door

and the iron gate,

preferring

to eat our meal without any breeze.

We know

that if Mrs. Ho discovers that we have

only vegetables and salty dried fish that evening,

the whole neighborhood

will also soon know.

thousands of colorful flags

We dry our clothes
by draping them on long bamboo poles
protruding out
of our kitchen windows.
So many colorful clothes hung out of
our apartment building,
flapping in the brisk sea breeze,
like the many international flags
at the United Nations building
in New York

that I have seen
in a schoolbook.

A kwailo tourist
in faded blue jeans
and a pair of dirty sneakers
puts his big camera case on the ground
and kneels in the middle of our narrow street,
his rear stuck up in the air.

His left eye squeezed shut,
his mouth twisted,
he struggles to find
the best angle
and focus on the thousand colorful flags.
Chaak, chaak, chaak—
he shoots the film
as fast as Ba Ba pumps
his sewing machine treadle.

My siblings and I giggle
at that funny kwailo,
and I wonder,

How do the kwailos dry their clothes?

typhoon

September.

Typhoon season.

When the radio announces

that Typhoon Mary is on its way to Hong Kong,

my siblings and I

are thrilled,

and pray for a very strong, high-level typhoon,

hoping that the radio

will announce:

"No school today!"

Lying in the bed the next morning,
limp like half-dead fish,
we all ask, "Do we have school today?"

After Ma says "Level-eight typhoon. No school today,"
we throw off our blankets and jump out of bed,
like half-dead fish revived in water.

My sister and I
clip clothespins to our earlobes
to look like dangling earrings.
I glue Ba Ba's empty thread spools,
one on each heel of our flip-flops,
to make high-heeled shoes.
And we walk with hips
swinging side to side,
like rich, sophisticated Hong Kong ladies.

What a fun day without homework!

tofu quilt

At the clothing shop
Ba Ba makes suits
for the American soldiers
who come on their ships to Hong Kong
from Vietnam.
Often Ba Ba will stay late at the shop
to meet deadlines while the ships are in port.

When the ships are gone,
there are not enough orders
for suits from the local people.

But Ba Ba has to stay at the shop,

waiting for his turn

with a customer.

Many of the workers

play mahjong,

gambling to kill time.

Ba Ba does not join them.

He cuts scraps of leftover fabric

into pieces as big as my palm

and as square as chunks of tofu.

He sews them,

one by one,

piece by piece,

into a big quilt

with different colors and

different textures.

I call it

a tofu quilt.

The quilts Ba Ba makes

are as warm as the ones

we buy in the store.

But his quilts do not look the same

as the ones from the store—

made from one big piece of material.

I don't want

anyone to see Ba Ba's quilts.

I often hide them

when my friends come

to our flat.

But the quilts from the store

don't have the same feel

as those made with

Ba Ba's labor of

love.

letter writer

I am the only one
who writes letters for Pau Pau
to Uncle Five,
who can't obtain a permit
to visit her in Hong Kong.
Pau Pau is too old to travel
to the Mainland to see her son.
But she misses Uncle Five very much.
She always thinks of him
and worries about him.

My cousin, who is in sixth grade,

often plays basketball on a court around the corner.

"A needle is growing in his rear,"

Pau Pau says

because he cannot sit still

long enough to write a letter.

Pau Pau always has the stationery,

envelopes, and pen

waiting neatly for me.

It makes me feel as if she is waiting

for a big, important man

instead of a girl of eight.

Pau Pau asks me to write down

what she wants to tell Uncle Five:

"Put on more clothes

because it is getting cold.

Always make your stomach full. . . ."
Even though Uncle Five is a grown man,
he is still her son.

She even trusts me to write down
secrets for Uncle Five
that I promise I will never tell.
I feel like a grown-up.

Pau Pau watches me write,
even though she can't tell
if I make a mistake.
She cannot read or write,
not even her own name.
But as I write,
her face beams and her eyes sparkle,
as if Uncle Five is
standing right
in front of her.

As soon as I finish,

Pau Pau asks me to read the letter back to her

to see if she forgot anything

before I begin to copy it neatly.

Pau Pau stretches her neck

and intently watches me write,

word for word,

as if she can correct me

if I copy it wrong

or remind me

if I miss a word.

Uncle Five always thanks me

because I am the only one

who tells him about Pau Pau

and the relatives in Hong Kong.

He also corrects my mistakes

and sends the letter back

for me to read,

along with his own letter written in

simple, neat characters.

When I see

Pau Pau's face glow

as I read Uncle Five's letter to her,

I feel so proud

to carry the safe messages

from Uncle Five

to her.

Pau Pau often praises me.

"Now I am not worried

you will starve when you grow up," she says.

"At least you can make a living

as a letter writer,

like the old man

who sets up his table

on the corner of the street."

I have never thought of

making a living.

I have never thought about being grown up.

I only want to see

Pau Pau's face beam.

report card

One day when I am in third grade,
I am walking home alone
on quiet Kennedy Road,
feeling low,
feeling blue,
afraid to go home.
I have failed math again
on the midterm exam.

Standing on the sidewalk,
I wait for several motorcycles to pass,

driven by white-uniformed,

white-gloved policemen.

A big, black car

with a Royal British emblem on the hood

follows behind,

and I see

someone in the backseat

waving at me,

smiling at me—

only me—

for I am the only person

standing there,

waiting to cross the road.

It is the governor of Hong Kong!

I cry out in amazement.

An important person,

the governor of Hong Kong,

has waved at *me,*

has smiled at *me*—

only me.

He must see something in me he likes

despite my poor math grade.

I feel big.

I feel tall.

I hurry home,

head raised high.

first cup of coffee

For breakfast I like to eat toast
with butter and condensed milk,
and drink a cup of Ovaltine.
But I also long to try a cup of coffee
to see what it tastes like.
Ba Ba says I have to wait
until I am a big girl
because coffee is a grown-up's drink.
I don't want to wait.
I beg Ba Ba for a cup of coffee
on my ninth birthday.

Ba Ba teases me, saying,

"Why are you so hardheaded?

When you want the wind, you must get the wind.

When you want the rain, you must get the rain!"

But he grants my wish.

I drink my first cup of coffee

in one big gulp

and have to lie in bed

for the rest of my birthday

with a stomachache.

In the evening

my eyelids feel heavy,

but I am still wide-awake.

I stare at the ceiling all night long,

waiting for dawn.

The next day in school

I fall asleep at my desk.

My teacher asks me,

"Are you sick?"

I don't remember

what I tell him

because I sleep,

my head on my arms,

for the rest of the class period.

It is my first cup of coffee,

and my last.

Now I know that the strong taste of coffee

is like the flavor of

dark-burned rice on the bottom of the wok.

flower market

In Victoria Park
on New Year's Eve,
fireworks light up the sky.
They are like flowers made of fire,
glowing in the dark.
Their noise,
like celebration gunshots,
reverberates throughout
the whole park, the air
smoky and gray with the smell of gunpowder
diffused in the cold night.

At one end of the park

are row after row of flower stands.

Our family, including Ba Ba,

who seldom can leave his work

to do things with us,

squeezes into the crowd,

so packed

that even water couldn't leak through.

We try to get to the front of the crowd

for a better look at the flowers.

There are blooms of all kinds:

peach flowers,

four-season plums,

water lilies,

kumquats—

all local, seasonal products of Hong Kong

from the New Territories,

brilliantly lit by the portable gas lamps.

Ba Ba wants to bargain

for a branch of peach blossoms,

but the vendor is stubborn.

He says, "No bargaining!

My flowers will be gone

before you can blink your eyes!"

Everyone

wants to take home

the best and freshest blooms

for good luck.

Ba Ba pays a high price

for a small branch of peach blossoms

and hopes that

it will bring us good luck

for the rest of the year.

jade street

Ma takes me for the first time
to Jade Street in Yau Ma Tei.
We try to find a good bargain on
jade pendants,
which we wear to bring us good luck.

Many jade vendors
display their goods—
Kwun Yums,
laughing Buddhas,
rings,

bangles,

bowls,

and carved animals

on the sidewalk.

So many, they dazzle my eyes.

I don't know

how to choose a piece of real jade.

Ma says that some of the apple green jade

has been injected with a special dye

to make it look like

the highest-quality jade,

and its color will fade away someday.

All of a sudden

I am more fascinated

with two men

who look like

they are playing a finger game

under a white handkerchief
while one of them is holding
a carved Kwun Yum.

I ask Ma why the men are acting so funny.
Ma says, "Oh, your eyes are sharp!
The men are jade dealers.
They exchange finger signs, bargaining over the price
under the white handkerchief
so that no one else
will know
the agreed-upon terms."

I am no longer interested in hunting for pendants.
I stand next to the men,
watching them play the finger game,
not daring to blink my eyes,
wishing I could figure out
their secret.

mr. wong's wonton stand

The first Saturday of each month,
after Ba Ba gets paid,
Ma always takes us out
to Mr. Wong's wonton stand
at the end of the alley near our building
to treat us
to a bowl of wonton
before we go to bed.

We are flattered,
for bald-headed Mr. Wong won't close

but keeps calling
"Fresh shrimp wontons!"
until we, the last customers to come,
have been served.

Mr. Wong makes us feel important.
He waits for us,
even on a dark, winter night.
He gives us the biggest wontons
with the most shrimp inside,
like steamed buns about to burst,
that he has made
just for us.

Mr. Wong refills the red vinegar bottle
because he knows
Ma will remind us
to drink a spoonful of it
to help our digestion

after we finish

the bowl of big wontons.

This is why

we all look forward to another payday—

for special service,

an unusual treat,

and the honor

that no one but the bald-headed

Mr. Wong gives us—

even though most of us are

girls.

mr. hon

My fourth-grade reading teacher, Mr. Hon,
the handsomest teacher of all, is very special.
He never punishes us like other teachers do
if we don't behave.
All he says is
"I will read you a story
if you all keep quiet."
The class at once calms down,
so quiet that we could hear a fly
whizzing by.

He reads us

a Chinese translation of a story

about three American boys from

a long time ago,

who rode a raft on the Mississippi River.

Mr. Hon reads us many stories

about other countries too.

He opens up the world

to me.

I am no longer like the frog

at the bottom of the well,

who can only see the sky

above the well.

And Mr. Hon is the *first* teacher

who displays my stories

marked "Great work!"

on the classroom bulletin board

even though

I

am

just

a

girl.

I wish, I wish

Ba Ba doesn't have enough work—
there are fewer ships bringing American soldiers
than there used to be.
Ma doesn't have many buttonholes
to sew by hand at home
since there are not many suits
being made.

Ma is short of cash to pay the rent,
the biggest expense from Ba Ba's income.
She even dumps out all our *lai see* money,

but still she doesn't have enough.

Ma leaves for a little while

to avoid seeing the landlord

when he comes to collect the rent

on the first day of the month.

I am the one who has to tell him,

"My ma is not home,

but she will give the rent to you soon."

Hearing the landlord curse,

I wish,

I wish

we could pay the rent

on time.

bargain street

Some Sunday afternoons in my fifth-grade year
I keep an eye on the customers
for Auntie Seven
when she sells leather handbags
at a well-known shopping street for tourists
in Central District.

Once in a while
I speak in my broken English
and tell the price of whatever the customers ask about.
They don't know

they can bargain,

as low as

one third of the asking price.

They pay what I say

and still think it is a good buy.

My auntie often says,

"Those stupid kwailos are being cheated

and don't even know it!"

I can tell

she is happy doing business

with the kwailos.

And so am I.

They are not

as picky as some of the local people,

who turn the piles of handbags

upside down

and still

don't buy anything

if they don't get a bargain

even lower than one third of the asking price.

Auntie Seven thanks me

and gives me ten dollars

each time I help her.

So much money

just for talking and bargaining!

what I want to be

Cousin Yee, Uncle Five's daughter,

gets a student permit

to come from the Mainland to Hong Kong

for a month's visit with Pau Pau.

I take her to Cheung Chau,

the island south of Hong Kong.

We lie on a big rock,

hand in hand,

on the quiet hill

next to the rocky shore.

We watch the white clouds drifting by

and listen to the birds greeting us

as they fly over us in the sky.

We listen to the waves

breaking on the rocks,

making a tremendous roar

like ten thousand horses stampeding on a battlefield.

I tell Cousin Yee how much

I like to eat dan lai.

And we tell each other secrets.

She tells me she wants to be a doctor

when she grows up.

I tell her I might sell handbags.

"A saleslady?" she gasps.

"No! You can be a writer!

You could recite classical poems

better than us when you were little.

You write

very good letters

to my ba ba."

"Writer?" I ask.

I have never met a writer.

I think a writer is someone

very far away,

out of touch and

unreal.

"Yes," Cousin Yee adds.

"And then you will have an excuse

to eat more dan lai,

if you become a writer."

I am puzzled.

How would being a writer

allow me to eat more dan lai?

Cousin Yee explains.

"Dan lai is made from milk.

Milk is protein, and

protein will strengthen your brain.

A writer must use her brain

to make up stories.

That's why

you will have an excuse

to eat more dan lai."

"I want to be a writer

so I can eat MORE dan lai!"

I shout with joy.

toss and turn

I cannot sleep that night
after I come back from Cheung Chau.
I toss and turn,
thinking of what I need to do
to become a writer.

I remember what Mr. Hon
always said:
"A writer must love books
and read a lot."

I do not own any books,

except for my textbooks.

I must find a way to make money

to buy some.

I think and think,

until I know what I am going to do.

big dream

The winter break of my fifth-grade year
I beg my ma to bring home
bags of plastic flower parts
from the piecework factory nearby.
I assemble them
into beautiful bouquets.
Though the stiff stems
hurt my fingers,
I don't complain.
I work past my bedtime
and wash my face

with cold water

to keep awake

to meet the factory's deadline.

Sometimes,

I ask Ma to go to another factory to bring home

bags of small metal toy cars.

On each one of them I paint

silver headlights and red taillights

and a silver racing stripe

down each side.

My hands cramp

from holding the brush too long,

and I sneeze

from the paint thinner.

Ma tells me to stop painting them.

Only a few dollars is not worth so much suffering.

But I refuse.

Ma does not understand: a little income

will accumulate into a big sum.

For I have

a big dream,

a big goal—being a writer.

When someone around the world

decorates with plastic flowers

that I have assembled

or plays with the small metal cars

that I have painted,

can that person know that

far away,

a girl in Hong Kong

has a dream as big as

the universe,

a hope as bright as

the sun?

my books

My friends often tease me,
because I spend all my money
on books,
nothing else.
They say,
"After you read them,
they are useless and will be covered with dust!"

I make covers for all the books I own,
fearing I will mess them up while I am reading them.
My friends ask,

"Why do you do it?
They're just books."

But my friends don't know
my books are my world,
my best companions.
Their stories make me cry,
make me laugh,
make me wonder,
and dream
that someday I will
read my *own* book.

the punishment

Math is so boring.
My fifth-grade math teacher
takes away my book
that I spent a lot of money on.
It's a translation of
Tom Sawyer,
which I read secretly
in the desk drawer,
not listening to him
solving math word problems.

I have to write this sentence

five hundred times with a brush:

I PROMISE I WILL CONCENTRATE ON MY LESSON.

I am glad my teacher forgets to ask my parents

to sign their names to the paper.

I write the punishment in secret.

My teacher returns the book to me

at the end of the semester

after I promise I will never

read in math class again.

How nice, how nice it would be

if there were only reading class.

secret wish

I remember Mr. Hon
once said that
a person should see more things
and open his eyes
if he wants to write a good story.

Ma cannot afford to send me off
to see things.
So I decide that
when I grow up,
I will *not* marry a doctor,

or a lawyer,

or a teacher,

or a businessman.

I will marry

a bus driver,

who can drive me everywhere

to see the world,

and it will be

free.

And he must look like

Mr. Hon.

gossip

At the end of the hall from our flat,
several grandmas, our neighbors, love to gather
right after their supper,
to cool off.

Mrs. Lo says
that the forehead of her grandson's girlfriend
is too low.
She fears that the girlfriend will not be generous
toward the Lo family if she
marries her grandson.

And her mouth is too big.

She fears that the girl will eat her grandson

into the poorhouse.

"The only thing we like,"

Mrs. Lo says,

"is that she has wide hips and is as strong as a cow.

She can have many babies

and make our family tree bloom!"

And that's why Mrs. Lo's heart goes up and down

like the bubbles in the rice pot.

She can't decide if she

approves of the marriage.

Mrs. Lee complains

that her grandson's wife,

who grew up in America,

doesn't get up early in the morning

to cook breakfast for her husband.

She spends time making herself pretty

and doesn't care if her husband

is tired and needs to rest.

She still tells him to do this or that for her,

as if he is a water buffalo.

"What good is it that she married

into our Lee family?

If she doesn't care about her own husband,

how can she care for the rest of us?"

And on and on they complain.

Ma says to me,

"Why don't you find your friends to play with

instead of sitting with the grandmas?"

Ma doesn't know that

this gossip

will enrich my horizons.

This is something I cannot find in books.

So no matter if I am riding on a bus,

or a tram

or the ferry,

I always

perk up my ears

for treasures.

forty

Mr. Yim, my sixth-grade reading teacher,
announces to the class,
"Listen to the worst story
in the class
by Yeung Ying!"
He reads out loud my writing assignment,
"Dream of the Mississippi River."
I wish there were a hole
under my seat
into which I could disappear
while my classmates laugh their heads off.

Mr. Yim roars,

"Yeung Ying!

Why do you write about things

you know nothing of?

Why don't you write about

what you know best?

You only deserve a forty.

It's the lowest grade I have ever

given a student!"

Now

I know

I can only be

a saleslady, selling handbags,

after all.

if

If I had a choice
I'd choose,
I'd choose
to do one hundred difficult
four-step math word problems
that I usually hate the most
instead of a single writing assignment.

If I had a choice
I wish,
I wish

there were no more

writing assignments to turn in.

Just let me

write what I please,

and nobody would be allowed

to read it

but

me.

uncle three

Uncle Three, Ba Ba's oldest brother,
the head of the Yeung family,
comes to visit us.
I hide next to the washroom to eavesdrop,
knowing his visit must be related to me
because I will finish primary school soon.
But I wish he would just leave me alone.

Uncle Three says,
"The main purpose of sending a girl
to school

is so she can read and write a letter,

and that is enough.

Any further schooling is a waste."

Ma says,

"It is *not* a waste.

Girls and boys are the same."

"They are not the same," Uncle Three says.

"What good is it for a girl

to have an education beyond primary school?

She will just be like you, burying herself

in the kitchen,

a yellow-faced, worn-out woman."

Ma's face turns as red as a rooster's comb.

She jumps to her feet,

like Taishan mountain, solid and strong.

She declares fearlessly,

"I will send her to junior high school,

even if the sky falls on top of me!"

Ba Ba gasps.

Uncle Three grits his teeth.

None of the other Yeungs would dare talk back

to the head of the family.

Turning his anger on Ba Ba,

Uncle Three blames him for failing to teach Ma

to be an obedient wife.

Ba Ba is afraid to say a word.

I wait until Uncle Three stomps out the door.

Then I come out from beside the washroom

and silently hug Ba Ba and Ma.

wong tai sin temple

Wong Tai Sin Temple

is a well-known temple in Hong Kong.

Uncle Three and his wife

go to the temple on the fifteenth of the month

and draw a fortune stick.

They haven't decided

whether their grandson

should study at Hong Kong University

or at a university in the United States.

Both universities have accepted him.

The fortune stick indicates

it will be good for their grandson

to study in America.

So their grandson

flies across the ocean

with all the Yeungs

giving him good wishes.

How I wish I were a boy.

turnaround

I sigh
when Mr. Lee, my seventh-grade teacher,
wants us to write something
about a family activity
as our writing assignment.

I write about our family outing
to the flower market on New Year's Eve.
The sounds and smells of Victoria Park
and all the interesting vendors
are still vivid in my mind.
I write my story without any hesitation.

A few days later

Mr. Lee enters the classroom

with a stack of our stories.

I cross my fingers.

As

Mr. Lee says

"Yeung Ying! I want to tell you . . . ,"

I hold my breath.

"Your story really comes to life."

Good or bad? I wonder,

until he says my story

is the best in the class.

I get a ninety-five,

the highest grade!

Thank you, Mr. Lee.

Now I like writing assignments again,

instead of math word problems.

mr. lee

Mr. Lee

writes on my paper about

the wonton man,

"You write very well.

Keep trying.

You can be a writer someday."

Those three sentences

make me blush, and

I would like to kowtow

to Mr. Lee.

He sees the talent

of a writer—

something far beyond the saleslady

I thought I had to be.

my diary

My diary

is not fancy.

It is just an inexpensive

exercise book.

Still, it is my secret companion.

I tell it the gossip I hear,

the things I see,

the things I do,

the dreams I have,

and how I feel.

I list the books I have read,

jot down notes about their authors,

and write down sentences that I like.

And I give all my entries

one hundred!

t r a m   r i d e

Back and forth from school,
I love to ride the electric tram.
I sit with my eyes closed
on the ride that takes forty-five minutes
one way.

The boxy green tram car
follows the track,
moving along smoothly,
right in the middle of the road
on Hong Kong Island.

The track twists and turns,
curve after curve, making the tram car
sway left and right.
It feels like
when my ma
gently rocked me
when I was little.

And the *ding ding* of the tram bell
sounds like my ma
softly singing me
a lullaby.

The tram is the best place
to let
my imagination
fly—
to make up stories
of my own.

lucky mirror

Several people on our hall
suddenly have bad luck.

In the flat to our left,
Mrs. Kong's mother-in-law,
who often complains
how badly Mrs. Kong is treating her,
dies.
Mrs. Kong has a nervous breakdown,
and no one knows why.

Old Mr. Tee,

who lives at the end of the corridor,

gets hurt

by a flowerpot falling

from someone's balcony

while he is coming home

from a morning walk.

In the dark I slip

on a banana peel

that someone has thrown on the concrete stairway,

and my tailbone hits right on the edge of the step.

It hurts so badly that

I think my back is breaking apart.

Ba Ba is the first one

to hang a lucky mirror outside,

over our doorframe,

to reflect back bad luck from other flats.

Soon all the doors

along our long hall

have lucky mirrors hanging over them.

Now the bad luck

will bounce

back and forth

like a Ping-Pong ball,

with no place to go,

no place to land.

The mirrors will keep us

lucky

all year long.

my new name

Lying on my bed
to rest my injured back,
I have again finished reading
Tom Sawyer.
With nothing else to do,
nowhere to go,
I write a story
about the tofu quilts
that Ba Ba makes.
I have already
outlined it in my mind

while riding the tram
to and from school.

I carefully copy my story onto
manuscript paper.
I give myself a pen name, Ma Ying,
thinking that it sounds a little
like Mark Twain.
Secretly I mail the story
to a weekly youth newspaper,
not wanting my family to know.
I fear they will laugh at me
if it isn't accepted.

I check the newspaper every week,
because the paper
does not notify authors
when their stories
will be published.

The story that I sent

seems to have disappeared,

like a rock

that has sunk to the bottom of the sea.

Then one day, three months later,

a classmate shows me

an article

about a story that

the editor has given high praise,

saying that the inner thoughts are great.

I glance at the writer's name

and don't recognize it at first

until I start reading the story.

I am startled.

It is *my* story!

I think becoming a published writer

is even easier than selling handbags.

All I need is paper and a pen!

But Ma and Ba Ba do not praise me to my face,

for that is not the Chinese way.

Instead, Ma promises me

a bowl of dan lai

whenever we go back to visit Uncle Five.

When I am not around,

Ma shows my published story to the relatives.

It stirs the whole Yeung clan.

I, a girl of twelve years, have earned a fee from writing.

I have done something

that no one else

in any of the Yeung families has ever done.

Uncle Three reads my story in silence.

He just mumbles,

"So bad she was a girl.

She would have made it

big later on if

she was a boy."

I will never wish to be a boy again.

I am very content

to be a girl.

I have a dream

and I have a new name—writer.

author's note

This free verse poetry collection reflects my writer's journey. It is based on my childhood in mainland China and in Hong Kong in the late 1950s through the 1960s. Starting at the age of eight, I was a popular letter writer for my relatives and neighbors in both the Mainland and Hong Kong. I wrote letters for my extended family until I got married in the early 1970s and moved to the United States.

After my first story was published when I was twelve years old, I became a freelance writer. From my junior high school years through college I wrote poems, prose, and ten-thousand-word short novels for magazines and newspapers. I used several different pen names for my works. I was too young to know that I should use only one pen name, and too inexperienced to know that I should save all my published materials. The money I earned from my writing was spent on books that were not required at school. I wrote only in Chinese because I didn't

The author (second from left) at age eleven, with her family.

know much English. I planned to write stories in Chinese for a living. That is why I studied Chinese literature in college.

I met my American husband, Phillip Russell, during my last year at Hong Kong Baptist College. After we married we moved to the United States. I helped put Phil through graduate school by working as a waitress at American and Chinese restaurants. At home, after work, I started to write our love story as his graduation present. Although my husband had lived in Hong Kong for less than two years, he had acquired some conversational Cantonese. But he couldn't read Chinese. Seeing him just flip through the hundreds of pages of manuscript I had written by hand in Chinese was very disappointing. I realized that no matter how beautiful my future stories might be, Phil couldn't read them and share his thoughts with me. So I made up my mind to learn to write in English.

Once we started a family, writing daily about my sons' activities was my most consistent opportunity to improve my English. I never imagined that the diaries I wrote about them would become precious birthday presents later. Taking classes at a public junior high school for more than a year after I became a mother of two young boys improved my English and gave me a glimpse of an American school. Trips to the public library with my sons allowed me to explore American children's literature. The richness of the picture books especially fascinated me.

When I was growing up, I often entertained my siblings and cousins with tales of my adventures in mainland China. They liked the stories I told. They were willing to do my chores for me so I would have more time to tell stories. My siblings and cousins didn't know that eventually I ran out of stories based on my own experiences and that I had to make up stories for them. They couldn't tell the difference. Years later, I thought, *If Chinese kids liked my stories, American kids would probably like them too.* That is why I keep writing about my childhood.

Ironically, I did not get to eat another bowl of dan lai until more than twenty years after my desire for dan lai sparked my interest in becoming a writer. While I lived in Hong Kong, I never went back to the town in mainland China where dan lai is most famous. As I grew older, I was busy with my schoolwork, my writing, and my social life. Eating another bowl of dan lai became less of a priority during that time. The first chance I had to return to the Mainland was in the early 1980s, after I had been living in the United States for many years. Since then I have visited that town several times, and each time I have eaten dan lai. Once I devoured four bowls in one sitting. It stunned my relatives.

At a party three years ago, a woman who had just found out I was an author asked me why I became a writer. I simply told her, "Because I wanted to eat a certain kind of food." She thought I was not being sincere, and she didn't speak with me for the rest of the evening. Who would have thought that a person's entire career could start with an innocent love of a dessert?

acknowledgments

I am grateful for the assistance of my husband, Phillip K. Russell, my first editor, who smooths out the English in my first drafts and who also acts as my technology person, helping me through my difficulties with the computer. He is my driver and companion when I go to speak at schools and conferences, both in the United States and abroad. "Thousands of Colorful Flags" in this collection is a portrait of him.

Jennifer Fox, Senior Editor at Lee & Low Books, organized the jumble of poems that I submitted into a more coherent theme and offered valuable insights into how I could make this book better. Louise E. May, Editor in Chief at Lee & Low, helped me polish the final drafts to get the manuscript into publishable form.

glossary

abacus (AH-buh-kuhs *or* ah-BAH-kuhs): device for making arithmetic calculations, consisting of a frame with rods on which counters or beads are moved

Ah Mah (ah mah): paternal grandmother

Ba Ba (bah bah): father

Buddha (BOO-duh): ancient Indian religious teacher; founder of Buddhism

Cantonese (KAN-tohn-eez *or* kan-teh-NEEZ): people from southern China who speak the Cantonese dialect. Most Cantonese people eat rice and fish as their staple foods and are usually smaller than people from northern China.

Central District: main shopping and financial center on Hong Kong Island

Cheung Chau (cheurng jau): small island south of Hong Kong Island

dan lai (dun lie): steamed custard made from milk and eggs

eyes of a suit: collar and lapels of a suit. These are the most difficult parts of a suit to make. When done well, they show the quality of the garment.

fireworks: Shooting off fireworks to get rid of bad luck
and bring in good luck is a common Chinese custom,
but in 1967 a small group of people used them to make
bombs and disturb the peace. After that the Hong Kong
government banned the use of fireworks. Instead, the radio
played the sound of fireworks during Chinese New Year.

flat: apartment

fortune sticks: short sticks of bamboo with numbers on
them. The sticks are shaken out from a bamboo container.
When one stick falls out, the person takes the stick to an
attendant who reads the message corresponding to the
number to find out the answer to the person's question.

Guangzhou (gwahng-jau): largest city in southeastern China;
near Hong Kong

Hong Kong: region in southeastern China consisting of
Hong Kong Island, Kowloon peninsula, nearby islands,
and the New Territories. It was a British Crown Colony
from 1842 until 1997.

jade: gemstone used for jewelry and ornaments; usually green,
but also found in many other colors

Kowloon (cow-loon): peninsula in southeastern China,
opposite Hong Kong Island

kowtow (COW-tau): to bow with the head on the ground as a sign of great respect

kumquat (KUHM-kwaht): small fruit like a miniature orange. When a kumquat tree blooms, the flowers are pure white.

kwailo (gwai-loh): slang term for *foreigner*, which means "foreign devil"

Kwun Yum (kwoon yum): goddess of mercy; also spelled Kwan Yin in Mandarin

lai see (lie see): money put in a red paper envelope to give away during New Year. Lai see can also be given for a birthday or as a wedding present.

like a bucket of water being poured out: In old Chinese tradition, when a woman marries, she becomes part of her husband's extended family and is lost to her own family.

lucky mirror: flat eight-sided mirror. A lucky mirror is believed to reflect evil spirits away from where it is placed. Some Chinese families in the United States also hang one in front of their doorframes.

mahjong (MAH-zhong *or* mah-ZHONG): game of Chinese origin played with tiles by four persons

Mainland: term people in Hong Kong use to refer to the People's Republic of China

New Territories: land north of Kowloon peninsula and Hong Kong Island granted to Great Britain by China in a ninety-nine-year lease, which ended in 1997

Pau Pau (paw paw): maternal grandmother

permit: It was extremely difficult for a Chinese citizen on the Mainland to get a permit from the government to visit Hong Kong, especially during Chairman Mao's era (1949–1976).

piecework factory: small factory in Hong Kong that sends out goods to be assembled or finished in a person's home. Taking in piecework is a popular way for Hong Kong housewives to make a little income at home. Pay is determined by how many units are finished.

primary school: elementary school up to grade six

sampan (SAM-pan): boat with a cover to protect passengers from wind or sunshine. Sampans are an important means of transportation in China and Hong Kong.

student permit: two-way permit for a student in mainland China to visit Hong Kong relatives during the summer or winter holidays

Taishan (tie-sahn): mountain in eastern China between Beijing and Shanghai; revered as solid, steady, strong, and powerful

three-inch tongue: popular phrase in Chinese; refers to a person who has a talent for persuasion or who usually wins arguments

tofu (TOH-foo): soft cheeselike food made from soybean milk

typhoon (tie-FOON): hurricane originating in the Pacific Ocean

Uncle Five: Chinese often use birth order to address elders, such as Uncle Five or Uncle Seven, instead of their first names.

Victoria Park: large park on Hong Kong Island

washroom: bathroom

wok: pan with curved bottom used to stir-fry food

Wong Tai Sin Temple (wong dai seen TEM-puhl): temple in the Wong Tai Sin area of Kowloon

wonton: filled dumpling, usually served boiled in soup or fried

Yau Ma Tei (yau mah day): district in Kowloon peninsula that has a typhoon shelter

yee wu (yee woo): musical instrument with two strings played with a bow like a violin

yellow-faced, worn-out woman: disrespectful Cantonese term for a housewife

Yeung Ying (yeurng ying): Yeung is the last name but goes first in Chinese tradition, with the given name following.